CATCHING THE BULLET

Catching the Bullet

AND OTHER STORIES

DANIEL HAWKES

Scarlet Tanager
BOOKS

Cover design by Andrea DuFlon, DuFlon Design.
Page design by Scott Perry, Archetype Typography.
Printed in USA.

Published by Scarlet Tanager Books
P.O. Box 20906
Oakland, CA 94620

Publisher's Cataloging-in-Publication
(Provided by Quality Books, Inc.)

Hawkes, Daniel, 1948-
    Catching the bullet : and other stories /
Daniel Hawkes. -- 1st ed.
    p. cm.
    LCCN: 99-95058
    ISBN: 0-9670224-1-X

    1. Sports--Fiction. 2. Young men--California--
Fiction. 3. California--Fiction. I. Title.

PS3558.A8168C38 1999   813'.54
                    QBI99-1332

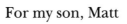

For my son, Matt

Contents

Catching the Bullet

Roy CURRAN GREW up sharing a room with his older brother Ted. Ted was an Athlete, capital A, and as Roy was geographically convenient, he became the Athlete's helper and, after a time, an athlete himself. Their sister Marley had a room to herself across the hall and kept her distance.

Mostly Roy caught balls from Ted. These balls would change with the changing of the leaves, the falling of the rain, the earlier and later darkening of the sky. And the better Roy got at catching, the more involved their pretend games got. Soon there were always only 10 seconds left on the clock or two out in the bottom of the ninth. The ball would inevitably drop over his shoulder into his hands for the game-winning touchdown, or inevitably drop and stick into the pocket of his glove, his heart pumping from the race to get to it. Inevitably, or they would do it over.

In no time at all Roy was good at sports. He was, without needing to think about it, the best athlete in his fourth grade class. So for his 10th birthday, Roy, with help from Ted, arranged a football game on a penned-in cow pasture at the bottom of the canyon beneath

1

their house, which their neighbor would for a few hours permit to become a playing field. Ted invited his best friend, Mike, to come and play quarterback for the other team. Roy invited all his friends at school who could catch or throw, or who would be willing to play on the line in a cow pasture.

Everything was set until he came out to the breakfast table that birthday morning to find Marlene, his sister, crying. "How come Ted gets to invite his friend to your birthday party and I don't get to invite somebody?" Her long auburn hair, which she had started wearing different ways over the previous months, was down today, disheveled, and the freckles on her flushed cheeks were bulging. Her thin lips were bent downward in a pout. Roy looked at his mother, who answered his questioning look with a shrug and look mirroring his, then they both looked at his sister. "Gosh, Marley," he said (life imitating art: *Leave It to Beaver* was then the most popular show on television), "I didn't think you played football. I didn't know you had any friends who could play. I didn't know you *wanted* to play. I didn't know you wanted to *be there!*" To himself, Roy thought, "Why should I worry about what my older sister wanted?" Other people, most prominently herself, took care of thinking about that. Marley had just turned 13 the previous September, not that she was ever easy to figure out before then.

"You *know* it's too late for me to ask a friend over now," she wailed, implying a premeditation beyond Roy's ken. "I hope your birthday is crummy! I hope you hurt yourself!" Now this was the sister he knew. "I hope you—" "Stop it!" their mother interrupted. "This is Roy's birthday, not yours! I didn't know you wanted to take part in this either until now. When I brought it up with you last week I got a big shrug as you disappeared into your room. Now I'm sure he'll let you invite a friend, and I'm sure he'll want you to play in the game." She looked at Roy meaningfully; his mother's version of subtlety was never hard for him to pick up.

"Well, if you really want to, I guess it's OK with me" (more Beaver).

"See what a nice little brother you've got?" In response, his sister threw him her best die-now look.

Her friend, it turned out, couldn't come to the party. "But I still want to play," she insisted, with an I'm-going-to-hold-this-over-you glare, after getting off the phone.

Roy must have seen her play before, but he couldn't remember if she had any coordination whatsoever. More and more she had taken to her room, so she was even less on his radar than she had been before, indoors or out. It was even hard for him to remember the last time she had done the once-ritual hair pull after his latest trip to the barbershop. Increasingly she was becoming Marley of the Closed Door.

It was soon clear that even if she weren't any good at football, she would be *there* this particular afternoon. As Roy's friends started arriving early in the afternoon, she actually greeted them all at the door, like a Mom: "Oh! Come in! Goodness, you boys are earlier than we expected." She actually said *goodness*.

3

His friends had not seen anything like this from someone remotely near their age. Then, as soon as they had sort of adjusted to Marley the Mature Hostess, she changed. "Bet I can beat you all down to the cow pasture."

She took off down the steep embankment through the prune trees with their red-orange November leaves, to the pasture turned football field. She was the winner, having mastered what all the boys on the farm knew, the art of careening, not-quite-falling while going full speed downhill through the mushy mustard grass and soft clods of dirt.

Roy never remembered her doing any of this before. Did she somehow fathom what he and his friends secretly took pride in, and master those activities herself? Did her locked room have an escape hatch out the wall, into the orchard, where she secretly practiced all the things they liked to do?

Ted and Mike came along a few minutes later, either not having heard the challenge or ignoring it. They went to the same school as Marlene; she was a known quantity to them. Roy's friends quieted as the two older boys approached: Ted, his brother, only 14 but over six feet, blond-haired, skinny but sturdy; his friend Mike not as tall but thick-chested and limbed, like a grown-up man.

They chose up sides. Roy's brother chose him, which didn't surprise him but made him feel great anyway. His sister's face grew longer as she went longer unpicked, but as the last boy was chosen, her face suddenly perked up with a malevolent idea. "O.K., that just means I get to pick my own side," she said. She picked Roy's team.

The game started. Roy got the kickoff from Mike, who was, as his brother advertised, the best kicker he had ever played against up till then. The force of the ball slamming against his chest stopped him in place for a moment, then made him take a step backward to recover his balance. But he got going up the field and outmaneuvered everyone except Mike, who by catching him and tackling him quite gently, informed Roy that he was faster than anyone Roy had played against before. Mike later became a college sprinter and ran one hundred yards in less than ten seconds. It would help if the future could tell you these things earlier, but it was enough for Roy to realize at the time that he was a rival for his brother. His catching Roy wasn't part of Roy's plan, which had Roy running and dodging, or catching those long looping passes from his brother, basically unmolested for touchdown after touchdown.

Roy caught one throw from Ted while pedaling toward the sidelines, another curling back toward him that he caught sliding on his knees. They were ready for something pretty. He took off down the field, hesitated as if to change direction, then accelerated again, straight down the field. Mike had come up to meet him when he hesitated, and Roy shot past him. He knew Mike would recover and quickly make up the distance, but in the meantime here was a moment of opportunity. Roy looked for the ball, his legs pumping, neck craned. There it was spinning beyond him, but maybe, maybe he could get to it. Out of respect for Mike, Ted had tossed it way out ahead, leading Roy to top speed.

The ball descended. He reached out for it but it sailed over his fingers — and right into his sister's arms. She carried it like a grocery bag, arms extended with both hands clutching the ball, walked the final two steps over the goal line, spiked the ball (the first time Roy had ever seen anyone do that), then picked it up and brought it over to him. "Here," she said, all perky, "this is what you were looking for."

Roy's teammates were cheering. But Roy was not pleased. "You weren't supposed to go out on that play!" he said to Marley, knocking the ball from her hands to the ground. "You were an ineligible receiver."

"So who's ineligible," she said. "No one said I couldn't go out for a pass. And besides, no one was guarding me." Before Roy could explain that no one was guarding her because it was against the rules for her to catch a pass, playing center, she had her response out of her mouth. "And besides, I've seen you boys play. You've got something where the center just picks up the ball and runs forward. If you can do that, why can't a center catch a pass?"

"Can't you play by the rules?"

"Can't you handle a girl playing the game?"

He knew that this wasn't the issue at all. His friends may not have acknowledged that there were girls in his class who were good, but they knew they were out there. What made Roy angry was that even on his birthday,

6

events were outside his control. He stared straight ahead in a combination trance-sulk for maybe half a minute. "Hey, Roy, we're ahead," Ted reminded him, coming up and grabbing the ball off the ground with a scraping noise. "Play defense!" he said, as if to remind Roy what was important.

When the game resumed, Mike threw a pass to one of Roy's classmates on the other team, Billy. A big mistake. Picked by the other team next to last, just before Roy's sister chose her own team, Billy was certifiably spastic. No one who knew him would have thrown him the ball, or even invited him to the game. But his mother and Roy's were friends. He reached out too low for the ball, misjudging its speed. The ball jumped off the top of his rigid fingers, up into the gray sky, and then down into Marley's snatching grasp. Carrying the ball comically like she had before, as if bearing a gift, she started running, goal-bound. Mike the sprinter gained on her, though not nearly as quickly as Roy would have thought. When he reached her, he pushed her right shoulder and side hard. Marley lurched to the ground and stayed there. Roy could see her shaking as he approached from the back. Everyone went still.

She was laughing. "You boys are so tough!" she teased Mike, who was starting to apologize.

"Are you hurt?" he asked.

"Not so you'd notice," she said, brushing at the mud freshly stuck on her pantlegs, then looking up at Mike. Then she threw the ball oh so gently at his crotch. A flirt ball.

So Roy's team had the ball again. After making a point of telling Marley, with exaggerated patience, to "stay in" and get in people's way rather than run down the field after she hiked the ball, Ted told Roy to be ready. Lined up far to his right, Roy was to take three steps forward, then cut at a right angle to his left and run parallel to the line of scrimmage. He would be running toward the middle of his field of vision, like a duck in a shooting gallery, entering a miniature stage from right, flowing toward the middle of the row.

It wasn't that his sister ignored his brother and didn't block, because she hadn't been doing that anyway. It's that Mike chose that moment to take advantage of Marley's flagrant violation of the rules. When Marley passed him on her way out after hiking, Mike ran past her on his first pass rush of the day.

Roy ran straight, then swiveled left. As he ran hard across the width of the field, his head turned back in expectation of the ball heading his way, he saw his brother freeze, obviously bothered. Feeling Mike closing in on him, Ted's entire body tensed, then hurried to release the ball. He had never planted his feet harder, nor had he ever cocked his right arm faster, nor had he ever released the ball with more forward thrust. Roy was about to catch the bullet.

Roy's brother had what might be called a rifle. Within another two years, by his sophomore year in high school, he would be able to throw a football over 70 yards. He could throw a baseball 90 miles an hour. He never played quarterback in high school — bad knees — but at the time he was in eighth grade, with most of his adult size and strength already in place. And Roy knew from their one-on-one games how competitive he was, that his friend rushing toward him would activate his adrenaline. All this was propelling the ball toward Roy.

He reached out but the ball crashed into his diaphragm before he could grasp it. He collapsed as if the general store had fallen on him.

No one can prepare you for having the wind knocked out of you. It was Roy's first Altered State. Instead of his life passing in front of him, the past converging on the imperiled present as though he were drowning, it was space that took on a different quality. He clutched for things, for people around him, but was walled off. In the grip of it, trying to grunt for air, seeing people's faces mirroring his distress and reaching their hands down to him, he felt far away, removed in his agony. He heard his brother's anxious instructions: "Shake it off, shake it off." He thought, "Is this the end?"

He must have been rolling, trying to cough, helpless to know what to do. Mud. Sky. Then his sister's face. It was up close to him, almost kissing him, her eyes wide, reaching way down into his. She must have been embracing him, to balance herself. He heard her voice coming over, calm. "I got you," she said. Again he struggled to breathe, his body straining, tense as a cocked bow. Then he could feel her hands at his back, pressing. "I got you." Then she smiled, from some place within her never revealed to him before. "Roy, it's your birthday."

If she had ever been tender toward him before, he couldn't recall it. Yet when she smiled, he smiled, and her hands, pressing, pulling against his back somehow forced some wind back into his lungs. Never had he felt happier about coughing in someone's face.

He wasn't sure if she had helped pull him up, but he was on his feet, hunched, his ribs aching. For the first time, he was thankful simply to breathe. Smudges of dirt decorated his pants, shirts, and hands. "Game over, boys, it's getting dark," Marley announced, scooping the ball off the ground. Turning to Roy, she said, "You're a mess," with exaggerated concern, and suddenly underhanded the ball toward his chest. It bounced off before he could react. "Oh, gee, sorry!" she said. Roy straightened up and started to laugh, and the laughter spread to his brother, who had come up to place a hand between Roy's shoulder blades, relieved not to have Roy on his conscience. The laughter was just loud enough to echo in the canyon for a moment, before dissolving into a familiar late afternoon breeze.

Marathoners

MURPHY AND I trained together for the Boston Marathon, back almost 20 years ago. Over to Fresh Pond, in the north end of Cambridge, was where we would go every morning, starting the middle of February. It was my first winter in the Northeast — I had come to Boston to do research on my doctorate in English. Murphy was "selling planters," as he told my roommates and me when we interviewed him as a prospective new member of the house two months earlier. No one really knew what he was doing, but everyone liked him just the same.

Over my vote — I had wanted someone we had interviewed just before him, who had been a conscientious objector, political — Murphy became our new roommate. For a few weeks he kept to himself, with the smoke emanating from his closed room (our ad for a roommate had insisted on a nonsmoker) the only sign that he was around. Then he began to emerge to watch football games with me. He mentioned during one of these games that he had tried graduate school for about a month and quit, and was working on a novel.

"A friend of a friend got me started with kayaking,"

he told me one afternoon. "In my book the main character is someone who loves the wash of water and air. The motion. Otherwise he won't be a bit like me. I'm doing whitewater with a friend of mine up in Maine, in April when everything thaws. Think you'd be interested? You've already bragged that you're a sporting type."

"Sounds too cold. But I'd like to be doing *something* before April. Especially with all the research I'm doing, I feel like some unexercised subterranean being."

"What about the Boston Marathon? Isn't that what everyone does around here in the spring?

He had told me that he had lived in Boston for just over a year, then had decided to break up with his girl friend. That's why he had answered our ad.

I left to go to California for a two-week January holiday. When I returned East, the first person I saw was Murphy. "Hey, good you came back. We had sorda decided to let your room out. See what kind of offers we could get for it. You want to match the best one?"

In two days we developed a friendship around topping each other. When he mentioned the Boston Marathon again, it seemed like a good New Year's resolution. Neither of us had run in anything close to the length of a marathon, though I had run some cross-country in high school. We were both up for the physical challenge, however, and we could use whatever conditioning we could get. For me it seemed a perfect complement to writing the thesis, a physical epic to match the mental.

I remember never being so cold, that first day at

Fresh Pond. Once around would be two and a half miles and we both assumed that being athletic we could do it virtually without lungs. We ran side by side, neither of us really knowing what we were doing, him running in sneakers I think he called "Jack Daniels" that were already worn through the toes, me in long underwear and two overwashed, threadbare sweat-shirts, revealing the underwear. I don't remember the make of my shoes. Only the thinnest sliver of musty leather protected my feet from the ground. The air was stinging me, my nose and lips already prickling, my breath starting to hurt. I started to push the air out of me, in a big "hunh," shuddering at the end of the exhalation.

Murphy turned toward me. "Shivering! That's good! That's your body telling you you're still alive! You sound like you're about to come." He was running out of breath trying to talk and run at the same time. Then we fell silent together for a spell, and I concentrated on keeping a metronome with my strides, one-two-three-four, one-two-three-four, as we turned around the lake, avoiding any slick-looking parts of the asphalt path, which were sure to be icy.

"Have you ever run this far," I asked, as we reached the marker indicating that we had completed two miles. The pond was beautiful, I began to notice, now that I wasn't so worried about finishing the circuit and having a pulverizingly cold walk back to the car. Tall pines and barren maples framed the path, fringing the blue-white solid water along the inside of our home stretch.

13

"Have you ever run this *cold?* And you need to remember that I haven't quite quit smoking yet."

That first training session was to be repeated for several weeks of mornings, with the distance lengthening, every muscle below our waists hardening and hating us for it. Afternoons I would take off for the Harvard or Boston Public Library in a state of righteous collapse, my brain unwilling to contend with 19th century English fiction or to pursue sources I would need, forever rereading the opening page of journal articles that would, I hoped, illuminate my developing argument. "The pursuit of the heroine in Victorian fiction." The only heroines I felt like pursuing were those female figures that placed themselves in front of me at least one to every library table, in that irresistible poised state of alert relaxation. Cognition gone, libido frustrated, I would limp back to the house after putting in the library time, several times arriving as a betoweled Murphy would be emerging from a bath, looking smugly warm and spent.

"Good day at the library? You've got to be the most thoroughly worked-out person I know. Do you have any *unambitious* projects?

Two months of this routine went by. About two weeks before the actual Marathon, we ran together in a real race, the Brighton mini-marathon, which turned out to be just under 10 miles. I had remembered from high school the running strategy at the beginning of a race, to go like hell for a quarter mile, just to make some room for yourself, then slip back into a pace where you weren't losing your breath. Murphy and I agreed that this would be the way to go. At the beginning the runners were packed together on all sides, so that at the sound of the starter's gun we were not only beginning to run but throwing off weight. Immediately I raced forward as hard as I could, but in only a few seconds I realized what I should have anticipated before. Everyone had the same strategy. After about a hundred yards of just trying to make a space to run in, I realized that the crowd of runners was moving right with me, was in fact bearing me along, faster than I wanted to run. The only sensation comparable that I've had was body surfing, with the wave propelling your ass along, and I felt the same salty taste in my mouth that I would get from the surf.

Murphy was no longer beside me, and we were only a few hundred yards into the race. I looked to both sides and behind me, but couldn't see him anywhere. I assumed he had gotten out in front. I picked up my pace right at the time that I should have been settling in to a speed more comfortable.

After a bit the pack started to thin out. I could feel myself working at my very limit, for two to three and then four miles. All the while I kept expecting to see him in the next pack of runners that I would then strain to reach. I finally started inching up to someone who from the back looked like Murphy, small, muscular, with a lifting undulation to his shoulders as he ran, the same faded green Boston Celtics sweatshirt and thinning red-brown hair. When I drew abreast of him it turned out to be someone else, someone at least 10 years older, in his late thirties, pronounced crow's feet around his eyes. Murphy would eventually get these.

"Have you seen someone who looks just like you, only ten years younger?" I puffed.

He laughed: "My lost youth?" He *was* like Murphy — I was impressed that he could muster cleverness; all I could manage was the thought that I was going out much too fast and would be unable to get through the second half of the race. Murphy the elder was actually just coasting along, and soon methodically drew away from me. Through the seventh and eighth mile, I was way past my second wind, through my third and fourth. Within a mile from the finish I spotted someone who was about 50 yards in front of me but laboring, I made him my target, hoping that in my effort to catch him I could ignore the conflagration in my lungs, as well as the ache that seemed to be growing in my right foot. We seemed to go slightly downhill as we approached the finish, and with it and my target runner in sight, I tried to determine if I had enough gas in my tank to make the effort. I was twenty, then ten yards behind him, then even, then the race was over.

I cannot remember if I defeated him, but I do remember my hands pressed against my sides, keeled over, being sick on the pavement behind the finish. When not heaving I would look back into the pack of runners finishing up. Fifteen, twenty minutes went by. Faces came across the finish, some relaxed, even smiling, others residing in torment. Finally I saw Murphy, his face set hard against himself, checking down periodically at his left leg, almost hopping on his right leg, his entire body braced rigidly away from his injured limb. He threw himself across the finish line, and stayed down while a crowd of people, me at the fringes, rushed up to assist. I asserted myself as a friend and pushed my way through. When I touched him on his shoulder, he knew who it was. "I was yelling for you at the beginning." He threw the words out, then suddenly sucked in his breath and grabbed his knee. The crowd around him, seeing I was there, backed away, and in a few seconds were gathered around a new race casualty lying prone just over the finish line. "I thought we were doing this together." His eyes locked on his knee, then closed tight against a renewal of pain.

Neither of us ended up running in the Boston Marathon. The ache in my foot turned out to be tendonitis and wouldn't get better as I continued to train. With a couple of days left before the race, knowing that I couldn't finish the distance, I stopped. Murphy's knee bothered him for the next six years. When we played tennis he would have to stop, massage and flex his knee, then continue, the same rigid look he had at the end of the Brighton race overcoming his face. I would beat him easily over and over again.

Three years later, we both for separate reasons had relocated to San Francisco and kept in touch. I thought of him as close to me, but I had been around him long enough to know that he had to be approached carefully. He still smoked, no longer surreptitiously.

One spring morning I suggested training for the Bay to Breakers. This was a relaxed San Francisco version of the Boston Marathon, only 7.7 miles. Murphy nodded at this, with decreasing vigor as he fought off a nicotine hack.

Murphy was working during the day, and I had been laid off from my teaching job. I ran with another friend from the neighborhood, Matt Olson. I trained with him on Bernal Hill, above the Mission District of S.F., and as we went around the far northern end of the hill, we would be treated to the widest view of San Francisco I had ever had on the ground. The Transamerica Building, Coit Tower, the Marina, South of Market. Running had never gathered in so much for me.

With only three weeks to go before the race, Murphy started to run with us. We shifted our training venue to Lake Merced, near the Olympic Club in San Francisco. With a wrap around his knee, he quickly got up to speed and distance, going twice around the four-mile circuit of the lake. Confident his knee would hold up, he started talking. "Do you know why they always had plenty of hot water for the showers at Alcatraz? They never wanted the inmates to get used to cold water and give them the idea that they could tolerate escape through the Bay. Didn't we sort of do that when we trained for Boston?"

We had heard all about Hayes Street Hill, the four-block rise two miles into the race, and we decided that we needed to run the course a week early, see what the fuss was all about, and know we could conquer it when we actually raced the following week.

We started early Sunday morning, at the precise time the actual race would begin one week later. We were absolutely alone at the beginning, on a Sunday morning, in an empty maritime area. Even though we were running easily, on the balls of our feet, we could hear the echo of our footfalls down the deserted street. After we turned off Spear Street and crossed Market, I could hear Murphy chanting one-two-three-four, as I had done in the Brighton race, breathing harder as we started up Hayes Street. "Remember when we were running back in Boston, and you were working so hard, doing your dissertation in the afternoon? I was so impressed that anyone could be so disciplined, so willing to put up" — he was interrupted by a car crossing in front of us at an intersection, the driver looking impatient with us as he sped through — "so willing to put up with all the labor."

I couldn't start talking, the effort of running requiring all my fuel. Murphy interpreted my silence as modesty. "Really, I know I spend a lot of time making you uncomfortable but I — ." Just then, as we reached the second-to-last intersection from the top, another car turned sharply in front of me and continued down the street. "Whoa there," Murphy said, grabbing me by the short sleeve. "I can see that suicide is your favorite way of avoiding conversation."

My hamstrings and calves burned as we churned up

the last block below the crest, which was Fell St. I thought about how my body was holding up, not wanting to engage Murphy, not having the energy to divert into the conversation. "How's your knee feeling?" I asked, saying all I could say.

"Oh, it's still attached. The orthopedics seem to help a lot." He had picked up on my unwillingness to talk and, deciding that this accorded with his mood, had gone silent.

Coming down the hill, done with what we expected to be the toughest part of the run, I felt my body relax, work confidently in automatic pilot, my breathing big and easy. I hear that trained runners don't get a second or third wind; such sensations are the province of the borderline in-condition folk, the favor extended to the sporadic runner, with the body feeling no self-resistance, concentration the simplest action in the world.

In this euphoria, I turned down Fell St., onto the Golden Gate Panhandle, and then, after a mile or so of that, into Golden Gate Park. I looked over at Murphy. His face was predictably battling against the sensations of limit. I expected him to stop, to give in to his lack of training. "O.K.?" I asked, knowing he wasn't. He looked at me balefully, as if a response would be yielding to all the arguments within his body to stop.

We finished the course, through the Park and all the way to the beach, locked carefully inside ourselves. The race was the following week, and we had proved to ourselves that we could do it. And we had been better off not talking.

We went over early the following Sunday, after training gingerly, sparsely during the week. The human collectivity on Spear St. was repellent, and we decided to go up the parallel street one block south, then join the other runners when we all turned right on Market St. The race started. Other runners had joined us but it was still far less congested than the actual course, and as we moved slowly we were able to get up to a brisk, comfortable pace without chopping our steps behind someone or feeling tailgaited by another. We turned right on Market and joined the flow. Now I felt crowded. I kept a close eye on Murphy, not wanting him to lose contact with me. My legs felt stiff, strong, my lungs a bit seared, my mind confident that I would find the next "wind." As we turned up the Hayes Street Hill, en masse the group broke into a loud, rhythmic clapping. I don't know whether this was a spontaneous response to immediate difficulty, but I do know there was a gathering in the silence between the hand claps, a sense of will summoning itself. You took on the strength of the group willing you up the hill — or maybe it was the strangeness of it, there in the inner city, the Western Addition ghetto, the absolute quiet between claps more powerful than impact, which was now like thunder as several thousand entered into it. Before I realized it, I was almost at the crest of the hill. Becoming conscious of my race again, I looked around first to my left, then turned my head right as I heard someone yell from there. A runner wearing a faded green A's shirt scowled at me, saying, "Drift into me and I'll run you over!"

Annoyed, I tried a reply but my lungs were spent, the communal exhilaration evaporated in an instant. I angled back out of the way to the left and reached the crest of the hill.

Murphy was gone. The runners in front of me braced themselves as they came down the hill, then turned left on Divisadero, then quickly right again, onto the Panhandle. I consciously slowed down, looking for the familiar face, turning from side to side. After more runners ran up my back, I decided to turn all the way around and run backwards for a while. I felt caught in the middle of traffic, in danger and causing danger. After about 30 seconds, I saw him working up to me, limping, his face dripping with sweat, without color. I turned around and ran along side, copying his rhythm, chopping my own strides to keep with him.

"You're O.K.," I offered, after longer than a full minute went by. "Just count your arms pumping, one-two-three-four, one-two-three-four."

He grunted, and we proceeded in step and silence for two miles, through the entrance to Golden Gate Park. Curving along on the gentle downhill, I could sense Murphy's stride lengthening, his footfall getting softer. "Much better," he said as we passed a couple of runners, one a woman in gelled red hair and black tights, showing off perfect hamstrings and calves.

"Maybe we're going a little too fast," he chuckled, angling his head, aiming his glance back toward the woman we had passed. Then he said, "Thanks back there, thanks. I needed that."

Soon we had come out of the park, and were at the beach, the finish line visible. The wind from the ocean pushed against us, but we knew we would make it to the end. It was time to exult in clean fragrant gulps of air and an opal sky, rarely seen above the fog along the beach.

In this celebratory mood I hadn't noticed that in the last mile we had become a magnet for other runners, catching up with three while two others caught up with us. In a tacit understanding, we all decided to go at the same speed for a good 10 blocks toward the end. No one slowed or accelerated, and I had the feeling of being borne along but not as in the Brighton race. Now I felt claustrophobic, coerced. Murphy, to my left, seemed comfortably a part of the others.

Then the leaders on the left and right of the little pack we had joined lengthened their stride, imperceptibly to the people watching, just enough so that the exertion and leg-consciousness that had eased within me running just with Murphy increased. Murphy went with them. "Come on!" the rhythm of their feet told me, but I fell out of step. The runners who had formed the box behind me now came abreast. My legs, responding to the challenge, pumped harder, banging madly against the pavement, the sand blowing up and attacking the corners of my eyes and nose. I would stay with them! Only 100 yards left.

I heard, before I felt, a tearing in my right leg, and I pitched forward almost on my face, my hands scraping on a small crop of gravel as they broke my fall an inch in front of the ground. Then it came on, sharp, then dull and big, as if I had been shot in the back of my knee. Something different, something final. I crawled to the side of the road, desperate not to have my right leg make contact with the road, other runners, anything. I looked at the runners pulling away from me. We had both caught the wave, only he would ride it all the way out. Murphy, Murphy, I know you're there. Where are you now?

Pants

THE MORNING GREG TOLBERT separated from his wife was completely anticlimactic. He didn't see her, she left no histrionic notes, or else they had become so routine Greg could only hear a cry of wolf in them now. She had left first, a bit early, taking their daughter to school, bidding him (still in bed) a cursory good-bye from the next room and leaving him a sinkful of breakfast dishes in gelid water. But Greg had always liked doing dishes, even though he had never admitted this to Irene, so if this was her way of getting back at him it had backfired.

Greg got up, dressed, ate Total corn flakes, finished off the coffee that Irene had forgotten to throw out, did those dishes, and left for work, a mere ten-minute drive away. "Boy, I'm going to miss this commute," he said, with almost smug regret as he pulled into Universal Engineering's parking lot. Remembering his plastic key card as he opened the door to his new teal Honda Accord, he was congratulating himself all the way up to the entrance for how much more alert he was, jolted into life. Up until the past month, when he finally made the decision to separate, every other day he would fail to remember the key card, looking helpless until a colleague came along and (illegally) let him in. He amused himself with more tidbits on his improvement since his decision (for example, how his hair seemed to be growing back on top) as he walked down the battle-ship gray hall to his office. Oscar Wilde, he remembered loftily, said divorce is made in heaven. His best friend Frank had been telling him how mismatched he and Irene had been, and Frank was the most perceptive person he knew.

He turned the corner into the alcove that held his office and was intercepted by Sarah, his fellow editor and next-office neighbor. He and Sarah had worked at the firm for five years together. She was not yet 40 and married to a man who worked in the Ace Hardware store down the street. Greg had just turned forty two months before.

"Glad you could finally make it in. Could you take this manuscript that Randall gave me?" Sarah asked, handing Greg an inch-thick sheath of papers, along with drawings and photographs that would be referred to in the manuscript.

"Um, OK.," Greg said, taking the papers and entering the office in front of Sarah, quickly scanning the front of his desk for any messages that had beaten him there that morning. "But you know that I have that Crayfield job to get to the print shop by 11:30 for a lunchtime presentation he's giving. "How soon does Randall need his job out?"

"Not until nine tomorrow morning, but I'm not going to be here after 2 o'clock this afternoon, and the

artists have to get started on the drawings for it soon —
some of them are pretty complicated. And Bill has to
find the negatives for those xeroxes in that package, we
need to make half-tones of those. I'll start everyone on
it this morning, but I need you to carry the ball this
afternoon."

Greg and Sarah were equal rank at work, and they
would laugh over people assuming he reported to
Sarah. But whether because of her greater seniority or
because she reminded him of his mother and older sister, he reflexively deferred to her.

"I'll take care of it," he said with as much masterful-
ness as he possibly could, and he was rewarded with a
quick, sweet smile from Sarah before she turned back
to her office.

He sat in his chair, thankful that no messages were
waiting for him. He wondered if maybe he could catch
a quick nap, just for a second while he was sitting down.
His office had that effect on him. It was a little four-
gray-walled Kansas at the geographic center of the company, without windows, cluttered with oversized desk,
MacIntosh Plus (at least two upgrades behind the latest-
model word processors), and large table pushed up
against the back wall. The table sported an old khaki
IBM Selectric in the center of paper clutter and in front
of two steel bookshelves, stuffed so thick with journals
and reports that they constantly threatened to fall on
the typewriter while it was on and vibrating.

The only direct use that the typewriter had, with the
computer now the main writing and editing tool, was to

write addresses on envelopes to other job possibilities. And Greg thought a lot about other job possibilities. On the wall behind was an Ansel Adams view of the Golden Gate, pre-Bridge, and a Diebenkorn "Cityscape," the olive greens and light browns mixing into the gunmetal of the office wall. A place one could easily feel trapped in, despite the *object d'art* that Greg hoped would suggest depth and sophistication. Other than Adams and Diebenkorn, the only other personality to the office was several pictures of his daughter, Megan.

The office was a monument to the old Greg, he felt. Now he would put more things up on the wall, or else make a concerted job search, not the half-assed checking of the Sunday Want Ads he had been doing. Things would be different.

"Knock, knock," he heard a voice say, and there in the door frame was Don Tulliver, one of the company engineers. Tall and slender, Don's eyes had crows feet that accompanied a slow smile. He was one of the people Greg like best in the company. His writing tended to be maniacally detailed, relying on microscopic fifteen-column tables spread out across the page and numbers consistently to the tenth decimal and beyond. His prose style was extravagantly wordy, with sentences that made Faulkner look like Hemingway. Still, Greg enjoyed him. For all his fussiness, Tulliver never blamed editors for not making sense. Between Greg and Sarah, Tulliver was known affectionately as Data Don.

"Hey, Greg, great work on the Terminator report; I don't know what I could have done without you," Don said with an inflected earnestness. Greg was not used to this from Don, but played along.

"Hey, Don, just doing my job," said Greg, in his most elaborately "professional" tone. "Have you been through one of those Japanese management training sessions, or have you just decided to become strangely complimentary on your own?"

"*Hai,*" Don said, with a clipped nod. Greg felt silly enough to break into the company song, if only the company had one (senior staff was purportedly working on it). He settled for a mocking "What can I do for you, sir?"

Don asked, still chuckling, "I just wanted to know how you were coming on that other job I brought in, the one for McDonnell Douglas."

Greg paused and looked at the textured-gray ceiling panels. "Was that the job you brought in while I was working on the presentation for O'Brien yesterday? I was trying to hustle that one out the door by Fed Ex time. When they give it to me 20 minutes before it's due, it gets my complete attention."

"No, this was a job I brought in two weeks ago. I told you I needed it by the 24th, which is tomorrow. There were about 50 pages to edit, and about 10 photos and tables that accompanied the text. You don't remember?" The burgeoning panic of the question raised the temperature in Greg's little office.

Greg started to fidget, his left-hand fingertips squeezing his glasses frames and resetting them on the top of his nose. "Well, let me think." When Greg trained his memory on two weeks ago, or any time in the recent past, what appeared in mind's eye was the look on Irene's face when he told her he wanted to leave. He had not wanted his problems at home to interfere with work, but he still couldn't remember any jobs coming in.

"Didn't you write it down, or make a work order for it?" Tulliver's voice rose in pitch and volume. Documentation was part of every engineer's training, and Greg could feel Tulliver's incredulity at his not being organized in the most basic of ways.

"I'm sure I did," Greg said uncertainly. "I'll go check with Elaine." Elaine Torrance was the department word processor. Overweight, whiny, dense, smoking-fast fingers, Elaine sometimes laid jobs aside without bothering to return them to Greg. He used to think this was subtle aggression on Elaine's part, but lately he felt he was giving her perhaps too much credit for devious behavior. After all, this was the same person who, when told that something was "six of one, half a dozen of the other," had responded in an exasperated, don't-ya-see tone, "But that's the same thing!"

Greg crossed the hall, hoping to find Tulliver's manuscript on Elaine's desk. Elaine was out of the room, on a break. Vexed, Greg foraged among the various stacks of paper on her dais, kept separate by paper clips, or by alternating "landscape" with "portrait" piles. He returned to his office, imaginary tail between his legs. "Look," he said to Tulliver, "if you've got a rough draft, or a diskette of your own, I'll get started on the editing.

Fifty pages I could do in two and a half hours, and as long as the drawings aren't too complicated, we could get those done before the end of the day."

Don Tulliver was still angry. "Well, in fact some of the drawings did need redoing, but I can see that they won't get done in time now. Yes, I do have the manuscript on diskette, and I'll bring it over to you in a few minutes. In the meantime, maybe you should start getting more alert to what's going on around you."

Don left Greg's office, a steaming scowl having replaced the smile he had brought in with him. Chastised, Greg spent the next two hours immersed in Tulliver's manuscript, stopping only to call Jeff Randall, whose job had been given him by Sarah. "When do you really need your job printed, Jeff?" Randall was notorious for giving false deadlines, setting a time several days before he actually needed it, thereby providing himself with a Pubs fuck-up margin. He had once told Greg (when Randall was making additions to his house) that construction workmen had to be treated like teenagers, watched over and nagged all the time. Now Pubs would be treated the same way by the rest of the company. To Greg, whose belief was that any incompetence within his department had preceded his tenure at the company, this was infuriating. He had himself to blame.

Randall admitted that in fact, he wouldn't need his job for another couple of days, but that "there would be no excuse" for not having it done then, given the extra time and that he had brought his job in early. Relieved, Greg hung up, after promising that the job would be ready on time. He returned with great energy to the Tulliver manuscript he had forgotten, giving a short lecture on the use of semicolons in the white space between the lines. It reminded him of his special expertise, if not his indispensability. He was the head of the unofficial Grammar Secret Police for the company.

Leaving his office to get a glass of water, Greg noticed Elaine, with her bovine waddle, carrying her salad into the word processor's room (she was "into Weightwatchers"). Lunch, he thought. I need to get my clothes over to my new apartment. He could bypass food today — seeing Elaine and her dainty salads nullified his appetite. Satisfied that he could get Tulliver's job done with an hour to spare that afternoon, Greg left the manuscript in a buff manila folder on his desk and sped to the door, managing successfully to get out before his boss Carl could see him and ask for "just one other thing" before lunch.

Once out the door, feeling like he had averted a crisis and was back on top of things, Greg felt another surge of self-satisfaction and in this happy state managed to activate the car alarm when his key turned to open the car door. Greg realized anew why these things were effective: he himself felt like fleeing, even from his own car. But he got a hold of himself long enough to click it off and head back to the house to get his stuff, the house that was no longer his.

Opening the door to the house, Greg found it different. He had never really noticed how dark the living room was. Ambient light shining through an atrium connected to the living room gave a greenish tinge to the couch, coffee table, and prints framed against a paneled wall. His favorite picture of himself, with his daughter, hung above the door into the hallway, a picture taken by his mother, with his chin resting on the palm of his hand and Megan pressing lightly against his shoulder, both of them stretched out and looking over some board game. A buoyancy emanated from the picture: the subjects were pleased to be close to each other, the intimacy somehow deepened by the shared enthusiasm for the game. It was clear that they liked each other in a physical way, and the game ensured each other's presence. The picture kept Greg home. It was the picture of family for him, and it didn't include his wife.

Finally, no one incident had prompted him to leave. Finally he knew, "Nothing at all is better than this." She was never at ease. She was smart, but was always comparing herself to her friends, and suffering by the comparison. She would cover her mouth when she laughed, sometimes even when she smiled. Her father never spoke to her kindly. In her mother's eyes she could never do enough. Her father habitually snapped at her mother ("This coffee tastes like shit" was the way he greeted her one morning Greg and Irene had stayed over.) No one ever offered any physical comfort.

Greg thought when he married that he could rescue Irene, supply the warmth that her parents could not muster. But over time it had turned out the other way: she was making *him* withdraw.

His friend Frank was the person whose company he

preferred, the person to whom he spoke his frustration. They enjoyed talking about books on the occult, the strangest movies. Greg loved Frank's zeal for the frontiers of things. And Frank had an impishness Greg loved. For a wedding present he had bought them a basketball. Now Greg couldn't remember why he and Irene had married.

Finally, exhausted with each other's shortcomings (Greg was not handy, did not have a feel for household projects), they had survived their last few years together in separate solitary confinement. They had made love maybe once every three months, perfectly predictable to one another, he knowing how to satisfy her, preparing her simultaneously for his successful climax inside her. They were expert at the mechanics of love, but the key ingredient was missing.

Greg broke his gaze away from the picture of him and his daughter, and walked down the hall into the bedroom. He needed to move his presentable shirts, pants, and jackets, out of the closet and into his trunk, and drive to his new apartment 20 minutes away. All this on his lunch hour, with maybe 15 minutes extra before his absence back at the office might bother someone.

Some of his "dead weight" wardrobe he would leave behind. He isolated the slightly torn short-sleeved shirts, along with the ones faded beyond pastel and the ones beginning to show unremovable discoloration under the arms and around the collar, putting those on the unofficial "stay" side, right next to the unofficial "her" side Irene had created the day they moved into the house. These discards he would trash or give to Goodwill over the weekend. He also left behind a light-weight gray suit that Irene had intimated was too travel-ing-salesmanish. It had never bothered him terribly; within two hours on the job at Universal Engineering he knew he could go back to the short sleeves, no tie, jeans, and sneakers of his previous high-tech job. Soon he had simply forgotten about the suit. He made him-self grin, thinking that he would leave the suit there as an ironic monument to Irene's taste.

So the suit joined the other stayers. Then he took the pants that his memory told him still fit, that succes-sive cleanings had not made too restrictive for his flesh-ing-out body, scrunched them together with the other valued clothes, and carried the mass of bulky fabric and coat hangers out to his car. Just to make the move more of a feat, he turned the key in the trunk with one hand, balanced the load with the other, and when the door rose, overhanded the burden into the already-cluttered back. "Next time, start earlier," he thought, "and get a garment bag." It took several slams for the trunk door to stay closed.

The trip up the freeway took 20 minutes. The street he turned left on after he had exited the freeway had the standard inner-city feel: high school kids, all Asian or black, going from the high school to the conve-nience stores across the street and back, playing chicken with the traffic on both sides. Greg turned left at Don's Liquor Store and then right down the street of the apartment building. Halfway down the street on the left side he spotted it, gray walls trimmed in blue, two spindly lemon trees out front. Clothes under one arm, he opened the outside entrance to Bishop Holt Apartments, walked down the stuffy, old-smelling carpeting, and let himself in to his new living quarters.

It was a one-bedroom apartment, with an extra large living room you walked right into from the front door (*Apartment without Foreplay*, he thought.) He looked at the floor, remembering why he had rented the place: a newly refinished hardwood floor gleamed blond, solid, immensely bare without furniture. A solitary red-topped card table serving as a temporary eating surface stood next to the door leading to the kitchen. His footfall echoed through the interior as he walked into the bedroom, making him realize that he needed some rugs to muffle his movement. The emptiness caught him up for a moment. "I guess it's O.K. for a while," he said aloud to the stark bedroom walls. He started back when he opened the bedroom closet, leaving the door open for air as he put his clothes down on the tiny twin bed he had moved in the previous weekend. Suddenly thirsty, he walked back through the living room into the kitchen, pausing to take his shoes off. There was a quart of milk by itself on the top shelf of the refrigerator, a can of Minute Maid orange juice in the freezer, a package of Dairy Gold butter-margarine in the refrigerator door. Greg hated shopping, but there was clearly no getting around it. He settled for a glass of water from the sink tap.

Walking back to the bedroom, more quietly without

shoes, he started putting the shirts, jackets, then pants onto the coat hanger rod. He realized as he finished putting the shirts away that he would have to get back to work soon, so he could not daydream about his new life in these surroundings, as he had done when he had moved in those few articles waiting for him today. But as he stored the last of what he wanted to hang up, he had the sense of getting through faster than he had expected. Perplexed, he went back through his shirts, separating them impatiently on the rod. Yes, they were all there. Then the jackets. Yes, there were only four of them, he couldn't have messed up there. But as he went through his pants, he realized that his pleated gray pants, the slacks that had gone best with the gray Harris Tweed jacket he liked to wear, were missing.

He tried to remember where he had put them. He knew he hadn't left them in the hall or front door closets back at the house. He checked in all of those before he had started cleaning out the bedroom closet back there.

He hadn't been aware of how much time this sudden panic had consumed, but he didn't have to check his watch to know that he would be late returning to work. *Fuck it. I'll have to go over to Frank's later, maybe I left them there.* He rushed out to his car, managing once again to activate the alarm.

Twenty minutes later, and thirty minutes later than he had originally allowed himself, he got back to his office. Within 10 seconds of sitting down, Carl popped into his doorway. "Got a minute?"

Carl was usually friendly and complimentary toward Greg's work but he did not look friendly now as he closed Greg's office door and took a chair next to him. "Greg, I'm not happy about what I heard. Don Tulliver spoke to me this morning and mentioned that you had forgotten about a job that he turned in several weeks ago. Could you explain how that happened?"

Greg could feel the vice around his neck, the color enter his face. "I don't remember him giving it to me."

Carl looked hard at Greg. "I count on you," he continued, "We don't get slack from anybody for anything. When the engineers are considerate enough to bring their work in early, we've got to get to work on it before it becomes a crisis. Otherwise they'll always bring stuff in at the last minute because that's the only way it can get our attention."

After Carl got up and left, Greg stared at nothing, ignored an incoming phone call, then held his forehead in his hands for a minute, elbows propped on his desk. "I need this!" he sighed to himself. "Nobody knows what's happening, and they shouldn't have to, but it's still not the day I want people coming at me."

He managed to clear these thoughts from his head, at least enough to get back on Tulliver's job and make progress. His forgetfulness still bothered him, for some reason the pants even more than Tulliver's job. He couldn't have forgotten anything so big, so obvious. Got to be at Frank's then; it's the only place where he even changed clothes (to play tennis and shower afterwards). And he needed someone to talk to anyway.

At 5:30, with people waving good-byes into his office, Greg phoned Frank. Frank seemed a little hesitant when Greg said he needed to come by, but said sure, come on up, have a beer. "Sounds like it's been kind of a long day."

Frank lived not far from Greg's new apartment, across the street from John Muir Park, where they would sometimes play tennis on the rare occasion that one of the three courts was empty. The two of them were good players, and as a doubles team they had been invited to the State tournament the year before, winning two matches before losing to the eventual champions.

Frank's perennial ambition, it occurred to Greg, was to be on top of the situation, like some knowing detective, Philip Marlowe and Travis McGhee rolled into one. Frank had gone to Yale and won the fiction prize there, but had never published anything. However dry his creative well had gone, his critical eye never stopped working. He had once found fault with Greg's posture driving a car. Greg had felt about five years old.

That was the worst of Frank, that nobody (including himself) could quite measure up. The best was that he and Greg could synchronize in a moment. They both looked for openings in every conversation. As if they were rallying in tennis, they would try to make each statement top the previous one, hitting it back with spin. Both were the most competitive people they knew.

"Hey," said Frank, smiling as he answered the door, "Work making you crazy?" He himself intermittently

39

worked at convention sites, putting up booths for trade shows, but this wasn't regular. His real vocation was playing the stock market. He was devoted to get-rich-quick schemes, once even telling Greg that he expected to be a millionaire by the time he was 35. He was now behind schedule by more than five years.

"Did I tell you that I moved my stuff today."

"So," he said after a pause, gesturing for Greg to take a seat on his tan couch at the end of his tiny, busy-looking living room. "would you like a beer.?" He would do this, Frank, delay serious subjects with a nonsequitur. Was it a nervousness with intimacy, or a refusal to say something weighty because nothing could sound fresh? Greg was in the habit of giving Frank the benefit of the doubt. With the offered beer and glass in hands, Greg sat back on the couch.

"Yeeaah," Frank exhaled, a signature opening, an expression that Greg had noticed with dismay was part of his own stock of expressions now. But Frank didn't elaborate, preferring instead to look silently at Greg with a poker face.

"You said we were the most mismatched couple you'd ever seen anyway, always at different speeds," Greg said, trying to get Frank to join in on the subject. But Frank wouldn't take the bait.

"You said something about a pair of pants over the phone. What was that about?" Frank asked.

"Oh," Greg laughed, "I thought I might have left a pair of gray slacks over here when I came over right from work to play tennis last Thursday."

Frank got up from his seat, got some matches from his bureau and lit a Marlboro, a habit left over from his broken-off attempts at writing. For once, he was the one who seemed fidgety, agitated. "Haven't seen any pants. Nothing you'd have would fit me anyway." Frank was six inches shorter than Greg, "neat and perky" a woman friend of Irene's had once called him. She and every other woman who had been interested in Frank had been driven off by his critical distance.

"Well, I looked all around the house before I took stuff out. I guess I expected them to be with the other clothes. I don't really have . . . "

"Irene really treated me well, Greg. I'll miss those barbecues we all had together," Frank broke in, looking at the wall, covered floor to ceiling with first edition books. Frank was a collector, with an eye toward discovering writers who would soon be big. It fit in with playing the stock market.

"It's not like I won't be seeing her anymore. We still have Megan together, we're bound to have contact, just to work out child care." Greg's words sounded automatic; what he was really thinking about was Frank's response. Why was Frank lamenting Irene? It was Frank who had suggested that Greg do something about his marriage. So Greg finally had. Now Frank seemed to suddenly shift his terrain.

Now he was looking at Greg again, more intensely than Greg could ever remember. "You know that fall when you went down to L.A., when you took that job at Hughes? Irene and I had an affair. I thought that I

41

would have to tell you sometime, but I didn't know when it would be. I thought once you left her would maybe be the time. Somehow if you left without knowing about Irene and me, then I would know you wouldn't be breaking up because of me. I didn't want to be involved in it."

The words threw Greg outside himself, he was suddenly a fly on the wall, watching the people that were he and his friend. He realized how myopic he had been. Now he had no coordinates. He saw how pale he looked, his eyes wide open. "Sorry," Frank said. "Maybe I shouldn't have told you."

Greg could not stay in the room. Unable to speak, he walked to the door, his knees shaky, his breathing loud and fast. He walked down red brick steps to the driveway, to his car. He remembered his car climbing a steep hill, then driving along a twisting road, as dusk was falling. Then driving through woods. Now he was walking on a dirt path in the woods. He would review all the things that had gotten him here, if only he could slow down, and if they could stay still. He felt the earth rotating on its axis. Two bicyclists and a long distance runner, legs spinning, passed him going the other direction. Looking at the horizon, the haze merging with the tops of hills and the sky, he saw that it would take time for him to locate things.

The Bells

THE STROLLER WAS collapsed in his left hand, the wheels bunched together, making a tight grip around the bars impossible. His right hand, arm, and shoulder braced against his two-year old son. "Damn, you're getting heavy." He plopped him down gently on the sidewalk as he opened the stroller, pulling the arms and stretching the legs till they snap-locked into place, then lurched to catch Jason with his free hand as the boy tried to sprint back into traffic coming down Bancroft. "We'll run when we get onto the campus — the grass." Staring at his father, the boy's eyes partly clouded, but he wasn't a crier and, after being strapped into the stroller, he resumed his signature position: middle and fourth fingers of his right hand in his mouth, left arm flopped over his head, left hand caressing his right earlobe. All systems go!

Jason did not ask why he was here, and his father could not have given him a clear answer. Mostly this was an expedition to get him and his father out of the house, a way of passing time until the appointment at the unemployment office later in the day. Having quit his job teaching at UCLA a few months before, Mark

Willis was . . . what? Taking care of his son while his wife taught kindergarten in Oakland? Taking computer classes at the local community college to make himself more employable? Taking checks from unemployment while he developed marketable skills? Such was his understocked store of responses to the inevitable What are you doing with yourself?

Father and son waded through the crowd of students walking toward the intersection of Bancroft and Telegraph, a sense of purpose and busyness leaping off them. Mark knew the feeling, having gone to school there more than a decade before. A friend of his who knew, said that this campus, more than any other place in the U.S., reminded him of a Latin American university, with the energy, the self-conscious apartness thick in the air.

Pushing the stroller toward the archway of Sather Gate, lifting the rubber wheels up over the raised wooden beams forming panels with gray cement blocks, Mark saw a young woman directly ahead focus her eyes briefly on the two of them, realize it was easier for her to deviate than them, and sidestep twice to the left, drawing up on her toes. She gave him an exasperated look as she quickly resumed full speed ahead. Oblivious to her impatience, Jason kept his fingers in their favorite places on his face, though he did crane his neck to catch a glimpse of a beagle playing frisbee behind him. Mark eased the stroller up over the rise, not really knowing where he wanted to go. He glanced to the right, up the paved-over hill, at Sather Tower, and as he looked at it, the tower shooting up, just the foot of it already at the end of a steep climb, the tower bell started tolling once, twice, all the way up to eleven times.

The eucalyptus grove would be just the thing, Mark decided. "Hey, Jase, once we get to the tall trees, we'll stop and get out of the stroller, we'll chase everything you can find." He could only see the back of Jason's perfectly round head and black hair when he was telling him this, but he imagined his expression as rather skeptical. Since chasing small animals was distinctly toddler's work, what's this "we" stuff, anyway?

They turned down a wide path, and it wasn't long before Mark had broken into a canter as the hill they were descending got suddenly steeper. The warm morning air rushed past, and he could hear Jason coo over their new speed. September often ran hot, and as they made their ascent up the other side of the arroyo, they could see young people sunning themselves, stacked up the side of the grassy hill. When they got close to the crest, just a few feet from the entrance to the building, Jason pointed at a girl smiling at them. She straightened up in a sitting position and moved her arms from one side to another, as high above her head as she could stretch. With hair to her waist the color of the sun, she was gorgeous, and Mark nearly drove the stroller off the path. Jason pushed his arms up from his head and moved them in precise mimicry, then brought them down to applaud his own effort. The girl laughed and joined in his applause. "What a funny kid!" Mark smiled at the girl, then leaned close to Jason's ear and said, "Glad you're having fun." They turned right to go around Life Sciences, then started down another hill which Mark knew would lead to a creek, and not long after to the eucalyptus grove.

What did he remember about the creek? He had walked this path his first date in college. He noticed Susan in his German class the first week of the semester, barely five feet tall, with a smile that (was it his imagination?) wouldn't quit when for whatever increasing number of reasons he would look in her direction. The instructor, Herr Ober, had assigned them German names the first day, believing that "being" German would help his students speak it. His new name (Jurgen) did give Mark a sense of disguise and possibility. Under the right circumstances, he could become anyone! Being "Jurgen" made it a lot easier to approach "Heidi."

He was seventeen, skinny, fresh off the farm (he had grown up on a Santa Clara Valley prune and apricot ranch, though he learned to edit out the prune part in his one-minute autobiographies), and powerfully shy. They walked together by the creek, calling each other sometimes by their German and sometimes by their real names, and trying *Deutsch zu übungen.* They walked by the Student Union, where three leather-jacketed black men with black berets stood on the steps to the entrance, listening to a speaker whose voice was being amplified from inside. He and Susan walked more slowly, avoiding eye contact with the black men. That's just about all he could remember from that night, except for Harry Belafonte doing a singalong with his audience, with specific age groups to come in at different times during "Matilda." Belafonte had called out "women over forty" to sing, and was greeted with a mock-stony silence.

Mark laughed out loud, startling himself and Jason. He stopped the stroller and started to explain to his son, when he realized that the eucalyptus trees were right in front of them. "O.K., this is where you get off," Mark said, and unbuckled Jason's stroller belt. Having been rocked to near-sleep by the pleasantly bumpy ride on the cement path, Jason got up out of the chair a bit wobbly and then looked at his father, wondering what the big deal was. He took Mark's hand for balance, then turned and looked over the immediate landscape. Almost on command, two seagulls landed on the ground close to the tree on Jason's left, and a squirrel, puffy from the generous leavings of adoring students ("how *cute*") came up to within six inches of the stroller, by his left ankle. Jason managed to see both the seagulls and the squirrel in one glance, and was transfixed. Which to chase? The squirrel was closer and gave the illusion of being more catchable, but the birds, he already knew, would produce nifty special effects if rushed ferociously enough.

Mark giggled at his son's dilemma. Then he took a few steps into the middle of the circle formed by the slender eucalyptus trunks. He looked up the long dark shafts, straight up to the converging tips of trees, at the top forming a green ring ablaze with light.

The ground was dry and he lay down against the trunk of one tree, reclining his head against a hard pillow of bark. On a similar brilliant day, many years before, he had come here with his friend Bob Eckert, after swallowing two mescaline tablets. He had met Bob in an English class his second year in college. They were the cleverest students in the class (Mark himself was the reticent Jekyl outside of class, the irrepressible Hyde inside), and therefore an enormous threat to their drone of a teacher. Lipscombe was as stubborn as he was tedious; the class's need to band together promoted friendship over rivalry.

They soon got together to listen to music, and they made each other laugh. Bob hadn't introduced Mark to marijuana, but Mark hadn't smoked it much before then, and never remembered it to be pleasurable before his times with Bob. Neither of them was a big user but the stuff practically *came* with the record albums, sort of like 3-D glasses inside a cereal box, an essential tool. And as the old Drug Scare movies of the Fifties so rightly warned, one thing led to another.

After downing the tablets, they started meandering around the school, expecting to feel some nausea that never came. What they did notice was how detached they felt from their surroundings. Mark ran into people he knew (an inevitable part of any drug experience he had) and was overcome with his distance from them. It was pleasantly hot, June, and he should have been feeling a lot better. "I don't feel a bit like flying," he complained to Bob. "I think we better get away from people.

Let's go over to the eucalyptus grove," Bob had said. Mark remembered this as though it just happened, but 15 years had gone by.

"Daddy" interrupted his reverie. Jason was suddenly over him, pushing against his right shoulder with his tiny left hand, trying seemingly to lift his father up, a look of concern on his face. Mark immediately wondered, his conscience flickering, how long he had been time-traveling. Guiltily he smiled at Jason, then grabbed him, making a snarling monster noise, and wrestled his son into reassurance. How much fun it was to make him laugh, and usually how easy! But Jason seemed less up for the game than normal, and within a minute Mark was simply holding on to him. Mark turned Jason face-forward, pulled him up against his chest, and resumed his dreaming position, with Jason's back against him. "See up the tree, up into the sky," Mark pointed with his free right hand. Most of the time Jason was hopelessly wiggly, but now he was still, just happy to be embraced, noisily sucking on his fingers in his Rube Goldberg fashion.

His boy's comforting weight upon him, Mark looked up, consciously trying to recapture what he had seen many years before. Then, whether from the mescaline or the glare of the sun, he had no depth perception, and the sense of space altering was powerful. The bottoms became the sides, going up meant going in, the bright blue opening at the top became the center. He thought of Uccello, obsessed with perspective, how he could make two dimensions look like three.

Now, looking up with Jason, he had a different memory. It wasn't so much of the visual effect in front of him, but of the person who had been with him, of Bob. He remembered Bob's wedding, six years later, for which he was best man. It was here he had met Laura, who would become his wife — stunning in jeans, a fan of mysteries. Bob and Karen's wedding was a three day dream, Mark flying in from rainy New Jersey where he was going to graduate school, spending three days within Bob and Karen's happiness, and striking up a massive crush of his own. For the next nine months he sent Laura letters, pouring in all the wit his dissertation-soaked brain could manage. By the time he got back to her nine months later, she was ready for him.

Jason suddenly shifted around, then started crying. Alarmed, struggling to his feet, Mark realized from the tell-tale aroma that Jason needed his diaper changed. Quickly he unbuttoned Jason's pants, pulled them down, pulled back the tape holding the old diaper against his thighs, and reached for the wipes contained on the tray underneath the stroller seat. As he cleaned him off, he noticed that his boy's forehead was several shades pinker than it usually was, and he felt another stab of guilt for holding him out in the sun, he didn't know how long. Would Laura be angry at him for letting Jason get sunburned? Irritated at Mark for not having found work, she frequently chided him for his forgetfulness with Jason. ("You've got him all day, he's your only job. Pay attention!")

Jason restored, they backtracked the way they came,

past the Life Sciences Building. Jason's beautiful admirer was gone. When Mark got to the benches near Dwinelle Hall, he remembered about the walkway going up by the Campanile and decided it would be faster to go back that way, past the women's gym, since his car was far up Bancroft. This route would also provide different scenery from what they saw coming in. So he turned up the hill, toward the Campanile tower. As he labored with the extra weight taken on by the stroller, one of his old English teachers, Joan Ackerman, was coming down the Wheeler Hall steps to his left with another woman. He slowed down but did not stop or walk toward her, not certain that he wanted her to see him. Was it worth activating all his self-justification tapes?

But her eye caught Jason, and she did stop, a look of delighted recognition on her face. "I saw a little boy two weeks ago," she said, turning to her friend, "who sucked his fingers in that same *involved* way." Up closer, she looked different. Lines encircled her eyes, and laugh lines had started on the corners of her mouth. In a classroom, she would often intercept herself with her own laughter, a hooting, abandoned sound that would make everyone laugh. Now her face lit up again as she looked down at Jason's face. "And he's gorgeous, what a special color! Eurasian babies are so beautiful. God, Ann, if you could only just have one — not without the preliminaries but without the waiting and birthing!"

That laugh again! Mark remembered her talking about the Wife of Bath, displaying her own gapped teeth to a lecture hall of 300 students to express her solidarity with lascivious women everywhere.

He took his senior honors seminar from her, and it was a wonder to him how interesting she had found his work. Looking at her now, 12 years later, he could not help thinking, "How important you are to me!" Smiling at him without recognition, she turned to hear her friend say something out of his earshot, and walked on.

"So many fans!" Mark said to the top of his boy's head, trying to ignore how abruptly empty he felt.

He could feel Jason's increased fatigue as he started the stroller up the hill. In front of him was the Campanile, and his gaze traveled up the tower, to the glassed-in viewing area about 10 stories up. He had not been to the top since the beginning of college, another hot September day 16 years before. He remembered how much Jason liked being up on his shoulders, how much command Jason felt from such a great height. "Let's do it, Jase, it won't take more than a few minutes. And you'll get to see the Bay Bridge!" Jason already knew and loved seeing the way to Grandma's house.

As they approached the entrance to the tower, Mark noticed the handlebars of the stroller had gotten slippery with his sweat. A sudden increase in weight was greater than the hill could account for, so he stopped a few feet short of the tower elevator and leaned forward, over Jason's shoulder, far enough so that he could see Jason's face. Yes, his eyes were closed and his mouth was open just wide enough for his right middle fingers to gain entry. Jason began to make the deep-wheeze noise that announced his nap. Well, since they were here, they might as well go up. His armpits were smoldering. The elevator attendant was a coffee-colored black man with a wrinkled face and yellow bow tie. "Nice day today. That's a tired fella you got there." he said to Mark. "Make way for the little guy," he said to the young woman who had preceded them into the elevator and was looking at a plaque on the elevator wall. While the elevator ascended, the young woman, her blond hair combed straight back, regarded Jason appraisingly, then let her face relax as she looked at Mark. "He's so beautiful," she said. "Your wife is . . . " "Korean," Mark finished the thought. "She's at work today," he added, immediately feeling silly for mentioning it.

The elevator stopped, and they all got out. Mark pushed the stroller up against one of the giant panoramic windows, then walked around the stroller to get closer to the glass himself. The two days before had been windy, so while this particular day was hot, there was very little smog, and you could see clearly the San Francisco skyline and Marin landscape as well. No wonder people came here, as his parents had from New York in the 40s. Nothing gave Mark a bigger sense of home than looking down on the bay.

He suddenly thought back to another time he was looking over the bay, above where he was now, from Panoramic Drive, with a friend of his from an encounter group back in the late 60s. Mark was the youngest of the group, just barely turned 20. The people in it were mostly graduate students in music and philosophy who prided themselves on being "active members of the counterculture." Much time was spent talking about exactly how you felt about each other and exactly who you were. The frank, spoken truth would set you free.

Of the six women and five men in the group, Sam was the one Mark remembered best. Barely a month older than Mark, Sam was in experience the oldest, seemingly wisest member of the group. He had grown up in Manhattan, had gone to Columbia at 16, dropped out and down to Mexico, spent time in India. At Berkeley he was by night a drug dealer, by day a student. And he looked different from everybody. This particular day that Mark remembered, Sam came into an English lecture class and sat down next to him. People regarded him apprehensively and not just because he had never appeared in class before. Sam's thick black Fu Manchu was complemented by lush black eyebrows growing together across the top of his nose. He wore intense blue bell bottoms that flared at the ankle enough to be a trip hazard for anyone walking by. Better than anyone Mark had seen before or since, Sam combined the look of sinister criminality and 60s laid-back acceptance of things. "I've got some really good shit here," he whispered to Mark. "Do you want to *do* some? Sam never *smoked* grass or cigarettes, he always *did* them. With Sam, the word seemed right: by comparison Mark had done so little, in the same amount of life.

A few minutes later, Mark had left the class with Sam and was driving along Panoramic, flowing through the switchback turns while taking hits from the joint Sam was offering him. As they approached the first turn-out vista point, right above the Lawrence Hall of Science, Sam suddenly reached out and touched Mark's right shoulder. "Take it," he said. They pulled in. After sitting without speaking, looking down at the water made small by distance, Mark looked over at Sam and found him crying. "My brother jumped off yesterday," Sam said, forcing the words, nodding out toward the bridge. "The cops told me. They said it was in the middle of a big traffic jam, some accident on the bridge. He just couldn't stand the waiting, he just couldn't take it. I wasn't close to him." He was silent. Mark looked out again at the city and hills, and then, closer to him, further down, the water.

The water looked no different now, 15 years later, from the Campanile tower. Becoming conscious, he looked around and noticed that the woman who had come up with them was gone. He and Jason were alone, and Jason was still sleeping. He pulled the stroller back from the window, turned and pushed it toward the elevator, only to find when they got there that the elevator had gone without them. The elevator man must not have seen them. *Shit, I'm going to be late for unemployment,* he realized. He looked at his watch, hoping that his fear wouldn't be confirmed. No, they were stranded.

And then came the sound.

Mark heard it with his entire upper body, a simultaneous blow to the chest, back, and head. Jason, who could not bear to hear a vacuum cleaner humming in an adjoining room and who was hard to wake once asleep, woke with a cry of pain. Mark reached out to grab him, while pulling the stroller up to his body. The sound struck again, a hammering explosion that made the whole room vibrate. Jason sobbed anew, clutching his father tightly, the stroller awkwardly dangling in air underneath him. In panic, Mark looked around for the stairs, *how do I get out of here.* At that moment he realized what the sound was: the chimes for the hour that could be heard all over the campus originated in the room not five feet away from him. It was noon, there would be more. "Daddy, do something!" the little boy screamed, covering his ears with his hands as a new concussion shook the room. Mark pulled him up to his shoulder with his right arm, at the same time detaching the stroller and trying to fold it up, at the same time walking toward an unmarked door that he hoped would be his way out. The chimes crashed again as he opened the door and found stairs descending. With Jason over his right shoulder, with the stroller under his left arm, Mark fled, while the bells went off above him. Time made palpable, time like a weapon, driving him down, down, down.

Rasslin

MY SON MARTY got me spending the better part of Saturday afternoons watching World Wrestling Federation on the Ted Turner station. And the better part of Saturday mornings, the TV replacing the alarm clock as my sleep interruption device. Come to think of it, the better part of every day, once he became precociously expert at taping things on the VCR.

I felt this was a step in the right direction. Marty, much like me at his age, tended to treat objective reality as an avoidable chore. At about three years old, he developed a cartoon habit from which both my wife and I tried, too violently it seems, to wean him. True to the child-raising law of physics, the more we steered him away from excessive television (*Hey Marty, let's play catch! Hey Marty, let's go for a nice walk!* or, as he grew older, even more hopelessly, *Hey Marty, help me get some of these big bad weeds out of the flower beds*), the more he would enter a walking pediatric coma. Sending him to his room for refusing to do anything other than watch TV only made everyone miserable.

Like many parents, we resorted to bribery. He did his homework, he did a few cursory tasks (like put his clothes on in the morning), we let him watch two hours of TV each day. So if you're asking the *Cosmo* magazine question, does passive aggression pay off, I say, just ask Marty.

I tried to do all the right things. To spend time with him, I started bringing stuff to read in front of the TV, joining Marty on the couch (*Move your feet, buddy*) and focusing on the page while he locked into *Teenage Mutant Ninja Turtles*. But even reading something as simple as the sports pages turned out to be impossible, for not only was Marty constantly rising and falling on the couch, in nervous rhythm to the action on the screen, but he tended to have the volume up loud enough so that he could hear what was going on from the bathroom at the other end of the house, should he for any reason need to get up and go.

In case you think by this point that I was a completely "dys" parent, I did indeed tell him quite often to turn the TV down. But I would notice that within 20 minutes the sound would be right back up where it was, even if I had stuffed the remote control down my shirt while I kept my hands free to read. All against-our-will cartoon watchers have discovered that the sound takes a quantum leap upward during commercials and then stays at that volume when the show resumes, to be jacked up further when the next commercial comes on (*we'll be right back in just a minute*) and kept at the new higher volume when the show resumes. It's like having an ever more audibly breathing electronic animal decide, yes, I might stay awhile in this domicile.

Years of this went by, years of auditory misery, years of waiting until Marty finally conked out. I had become much too savvy over time to actually come right out with it, but on some dog frequency my pleading might have been heard: *Get away from cartoons, get interested in human beings, my son.*

Wrestling wasn't cartoons: it was real people (acting like cartoon characters). So Marty's interest in the WWF, which blossomed soon after he turned 10, could be thought of as a transitional phase, the first of a succession of locks that would eventually take him up to the roiling open sea of adulthood.

It was a good medium for getting to know him. "Watch, Dad, this guy's really weird. You'll like him!" he said one day, pointing with his entire body — head, shoulders, toes rising — toward the screen. I watched someone called The Undertaker stride into the ring, on each side of him a dark-skinned young woman with bare midriff and heavily made-up face (the WWF never met a stereotype it didn't like), oboe music crackling through a low-tech sound system. I congratulated myself on Marty's new powers of observation, shown by his distinguishing what *weird* was and knowing I would like it.

It was a short step from my granting approval to his watching wrestling to his seizing on it as something we could do together. So my 40-somethingth birthday present from him was a trip to the Oakland Coliseum (I paid) to see these guys in their pumped-up flesh.

I had been to the Coliseum before, for basketball games, and was not prepared for how different the place would be for this event. Instead of the crowd rising all the way to the roofline, it filled approximately half the space, but all of the bottom tiers. I saw this as creating an illusion of crowdedness for TV cameras that would never pan beyond the top row of people. We were gathered round, participating in a visual fraud. Finding our seats, Marty and I crossed in front of a large white-haired black woman wrapped in a black Raiders jacket, completely attentive to the ring. She pulled her black-trousered knees back just enough for us to get by, her eyes never leaving the center of the arena, where the first combatants were about to go at it.

The ring announcer presented them and the show began. "Show," it turned out, was too strong a word. These were the goons in training for WWF, the undercarders who hoped to develop enough inspiring fake moves or gimmicks to be part of the televised show. There wasn't even a clear bad guy between the two of them. White Trunks attempted a menacing scowl several times, but only succeeded in looking like he was posing for his driver's license photo. Black Trunks merely circled backwards around the ring, occasionally met White Trunks in the center for a warm embrace, then started circling again. The woman next to us pulled some black yarn out of her jacket and started knitting.

Also, while they were big guys, their muscles weren't defined enough by WWF standards. I bet Marty (even he was getting a little restless, enough to let his attention drift back to me) that once any of these guys

showed they could be stars, their bodies would immediately become chiseled. He became defensive. "I know
what you're thinking, Dad, *and it's not true.* These guys
do not take drugs. Gorilla Monsoon, the announcer on
TV, said so. He knows, he was a wrestler back when you
were a kid — remember him? — and *he would not lie.*
He's the good guy announcer, not like Bobby Heenan.
Gorilla says that they drink this stuff called Ico Pro, it's
full of . . . good stuff, Dad. I trust Gorilla. He says these
guys are *clean.*"

Marty looked at me. He had learned what my raised-
eyebrow response meant. He had also learned how to
imitate me when I didn't want the conversation to continue in a certain vein. "Trust me," he said, with his best
paternal voice.

After another bout with another set of stiffs, I started
watching the clock, the sort of thing I did at Marty's age
as a bad class dragged on. I did notice, by the way, that
each of these preliminary matches took exactly 17 minutes, eternities both of them.

"Ladies and Gentleman, Michael Tatanka." The next
match was about to begin, and the announcer, suddenly
sporting a red bow tie, brought me out of my reverie.
The TV cameras were rolling, the main eventers were
now ready. Tatanka was someone I had remembered
from my Quality Time with Marty in front of the tube, a
good-guy Native American wrestler who sounded rea-
sonably intelligent, did not brag reflexively when interviewed, and only did war whoops because you had to
have your thing in the WWF.

His opponent, Shawn Michaels, was also famous. Everyone booed, first at the sight of him, then afresh when the announcer introduced him. It was not just his looks — blond, huge-headed, steroidal Nazi — but also his demeanor, which was paradoxically craven. Whenever Michaels was touched, which happens fairly often even in the worst of wrestling matches, he would recoil violently, a stricken look on his face, and look at the referee pleadingly, hoping for some reprimand against his opponent. He looked like a schoolkid who had found out that corporal punishment had been outlawed and was hoping that his least favorite teacher would be brought to justice under this edict. When the referee was unmoved, Michaels left the ring.

Leaving the ring is not by a long shot quitting in the WWF. There's a padded area running outside and below the ropes, an outer square where wrestlers often go not only if they're hurled out of the ring but also to regroup. For the bad guys, this is a strategically useful place from which to suddenly pop up, reciprocate abuse from the crowd, and roam around unseen (if an *agent provocateur* in the crowd creates a diversion, if the opponent goes along with it and allows himself to be diverted). It adds a further element of dirty low-downness wrestling fans cannot do without.

All of these observations were offered to Marty in the manner of a helpful father: not too much insight at one time, with an encouraging tone suggesting that he could be led to the correct conclusions about things. He ignored me. Finally, after another of my gently offered pearls, he turned sharply toward me, then checked himself and sighed. "Just get into it," he said.

Michaels spent a minute circling the ring from outside, his head sticking up over the raised ring floor like a curly blond periscope, looking wounded, gesturing evilly at the crowd. I glanced at the woman next to me, perhaps hoping that she could be a model of fan behavior for me. She had taken off her Raiders jacket, revealing a tan sleeveless blouse and bulky dark brown arms. They jiggled as she shook the jacket at Michaels. "Get back in there, Bleach Boy. Get in there, you ofay coward."

I laughed at her *mot* and she abruptly turned toward me. Sternly she interrogated me with her eyes for a full three seconds, then she broke into a grin that made me laugh again. "You heard what your boy said — get into it!" she advised.

And when I refocused on the ring, my loftiness had somehow evaporated. Maybe Michaels suddenly became all the surf thugs of my California youth. In any case, out of nowhere, my contempt for him had arrived. "Bleach Boy!"

The moment before he was to be disqualified for being out of the ring too long (even the WWF has its limits) Michaels managed to catch Tatanka talking to someone in the crowd, jump into the ring behind him, and throw an elbow apparently to Tatanka's chin. Tatanka shot to the floor. Michaels jumped on top of him, and the referee jumped down alongside them. Temple to the mat, watching to see that Tatanka's shoulders stayed in contact with the ring floor, the referee extended his right arm and brought his palm down hard on the fawn-colored surface. Once, twice, three times.

Pin! "No!" I shouted, as Michaels pranced around the ring, the crowd's shocked silence allowing me to hear myself. "They can't allow that!" I said to Marty, who then started booing with the rest of the crowd. Michaels stepped out of the ring and strode down the aisle with his munchkin handlers, his arms raised over his head in the self-salute made famous by Richard Nixon. "It's not fair," I repeated to Marty, who continued to boo. "They can't allow stuff that's, that's . . . against the rules!"

A smile grew slowly on his face. "What rules?" Marty replied. "How else are bad guys going to win except by being bad guys?"

That stopped me. "You asked me to get into it, so I'm into it; you can't change the game now. You can't have a game unless there are rules that people follow."

To his now truly mischievous smile he added a world-weary shrug. "Shit happens, Dad."

DANIEL HAWKES has taught at UCLA and Rutgers University (where he received his Ph.D. in English) and now lives in the San Francisco Bay Area where he grew up. He is a science and technical writer/editor at the Lawrence Berkeley National Laboratory.